With thanks to Joff, with love to Josh, Flan, Zach and Hetty
E.H.

Special thanks to Steve and Oliver
A.R.

RAINY DAY
A PICTURE CORGI BOOK : 0 552 545988

First published in Great Britain by Doubleday, a division of Transworld Publishers

PRINTING HISTORY
Doubleday edition published 2000
Picture Corgi edition published 2001

1 3 5 7 9 10 8 6 4 2

Text copyright © Emma Haughton, 2000
Illustrations copyright © Angelo Rinaldi, 2000

Designed by Ian Butterworth

The right of Emma Haughton to be identified as the author and of Angelo Rinaldi as
the illustrator of this work has been asserted in accordance with the Copyright,
Designs and Patents Act 1988

Picture Corgi Books are published by Transworld Publishers,
61-63 Uxbridge Road, London W5 5SA,
a division of The Random House Group Ltd,
in Australia by Random House Australia (Pty) Ltd,
20 Alfred Street, Milsons Point, Sydney, NSW 2061,
in New Zealand by Random House New Zealand Ltd,
18 Poland Road, Glenfield, Auckland 10,
and in South Africa by Random House (Pty) Ltd,
Endulini, 5A Jubilee Road, Parktown 2193

Printed in Singapore

www.booksattransworld.co.uk/childrens

Rainy Day

Emma Haughton *Illustrated by* Angelo Rinaldi

Picture Corgi Books

The morning of the visit it began to rain. Ned sat in his dad's new apartment, watching the first splash of drops on the window. One by one they fell, fatter and faster, until he could hardly see through to the shops across the street.

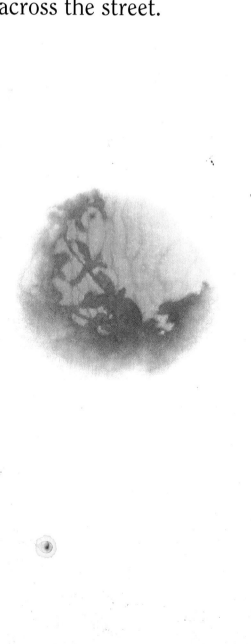

"Looks like the fair will have to wait till next week," said Dad.

"But you promised," said Ned.

"I'm sorry," said Dad. He put a hand on Ned's shoulder. "I was looking forward to it too, you know."

Ned shrugged and said nothing. He leaned his head against the window. It felt cold and hard. Rain drops trickled down the glass.

Dad grabbed Ned's coat and dropped it in his lap.

"Come on," he said. "We're off."

"Where?" asked Ned, not moving.

"I don't know," said Dad. "We'll see."

Down on the street cars hissed past, water spraying up from their wheels. An old man struggled with an umbrella in the wind.

A baby peered at Ned through the plastic bubble over its pushchair.

Ned walked slowly, trying to keep his feet dry. Dad stopped and waited.

"Hang on," he said, and dived into a shop. He came out with a pair of rubber boots. "Try these." He pulled off Ned's shoes.

Ned scowled. "Too big."

Dad pressed the toes. "They'll do."

Ned stamped in every pavement puddle, splashing dirty water everywhere. His jeans clung to his legs, cold and clammy.

Suddenly the rain got heavier, hurtling out of the sky and stinging Ned's cheeks. His hair began to drip into his eyes.

Everywhere people dashed for cover, but Dad strode on.

When Ned turned into the park, Dad was waiting.

"Look." He pointed to a trickle of rain water running down through the trees. "A stream."

He picked up a stick and started to clear the leaves from its path. The water rushed and danced ahead. Ned ran to keep up.

"Here!" shouted Ned.

By the drain there was a large tangle of twigs and leaves. With a quick flick of his stick, Dad broke through the dam. The water surged forward and gurgled into the black, echoey depths below.

They followed the path down through the trees as it curved towards the sea. A dog bounded out of nowhere and jumped up to lick Ned's face. Its damp fur smelled of old carpets.

"Jessie!" yelled its owner, and tugged it away, but the dog broke free and skidded off into the downpour.

"You OK?" asked Dad, brushing the mud from Ned's coat.

Ned nodded. "Can we go and look at the sea?"

"Sure," said Dad. "Let's go."

The sea front was empty. Clouds raced across
the bay, the air smelled salty fresh. Waves swelled
and heaved and crashed against the sea wall,
sending plumes of spray onto the promenade. They
stood by the edge, dodging the water as it flew up
around them. Ned laughed when
Dad didn't get away in time.

Tired and soaked, they sat on a bench and watched the puddles of rain and spray flow back into the sea.

"Hungry?" asked Dad.

"Starving," said Ned.

Dad reached in his pocket and pulled out a packet of biscuits. Most were broken, but they still tasted good.

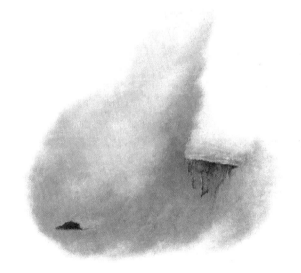

Dad looked at Ned's wet trousers
and muddy coat.

"Look at the state of you," he said.
"Your mum will kill me."

"She won't mind," said Ned,
trying not to shiver, "as long as I'm
all right."

"And are you?" asked Dad.

Suddenly the sun broke through the cover of grey.
The seagulls began to scream and swoop.
The tips of the waves sparkled in the bright light.
Ned blinked. "I miss you," he said.
"Me too," said Dad. "All the time."
He turned and gave Ned a long, hard squeeze.

"Things will get better," said Dad, "I promise."
Ned smiled. "I know," he said. "Rainy days aren't
so bad. And they don't last for ever."